THE THREE LITTLE BASS AND THE BIG BAD GAR

BY

JAMES MILLER

ILLUSTRATED BY KRIS TAFT MILLER

This book is dedicated to

my Mommy,
because she is my inspiration.

ktdesignllc.com • printdesignsbykris.com

ISBN: 9781096241409
Imprint: Independently published

Author: James R. Miller
Cover Design & Illustrator: Kris Taft Miller

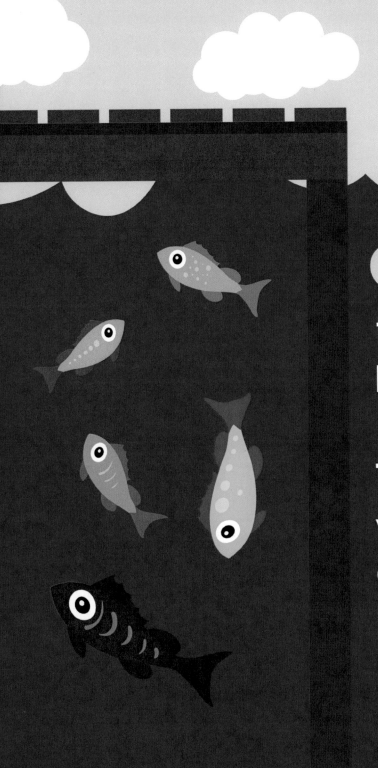

Once upon a time, there were **THREE** little bass fish.

They lived together with their mom and dad under a dock on Little Lake Gaston.

One day the **THREE** young bass fish had grown old enough to go off and explore the lake on their own. They each set off to build their own homes.

Bass number ONE decided to make his house out of mud from the bottom of the lake.

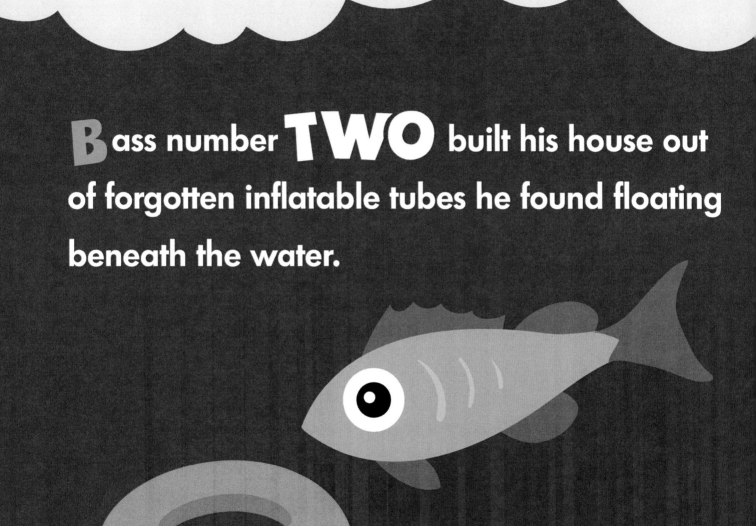

Bass number **TWO** built his house out of forgotten inflatable tubes he found floating beneath the water.

Bass number **THREE** took his time to think about what would make the best and safest home.

His brothers laughed at how long he was taking to make his house.

Bass number **THREE** finally decided the best way to make a safe house for himself was using rocks.

So he set off to collect as many rocks as he could which took him a **LONG LONG LONG** time.

His brothers laughed at him again as they sat in their finished houses.

Finally, his house of rocks was finished!

One day, the **BIG BAD GAR** fish came swimming around. He went to the home of little bass fish number **ONE** and bubbled...

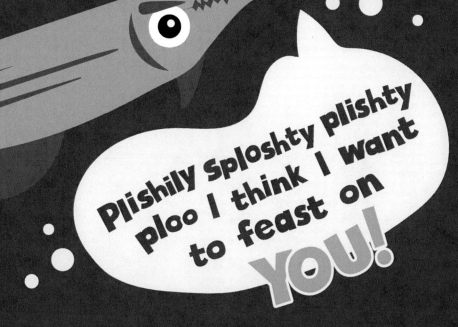

Plishily splishty plishty ploo I think I want to feast on **YOU!**

Little bass fish number **ONE** answered...

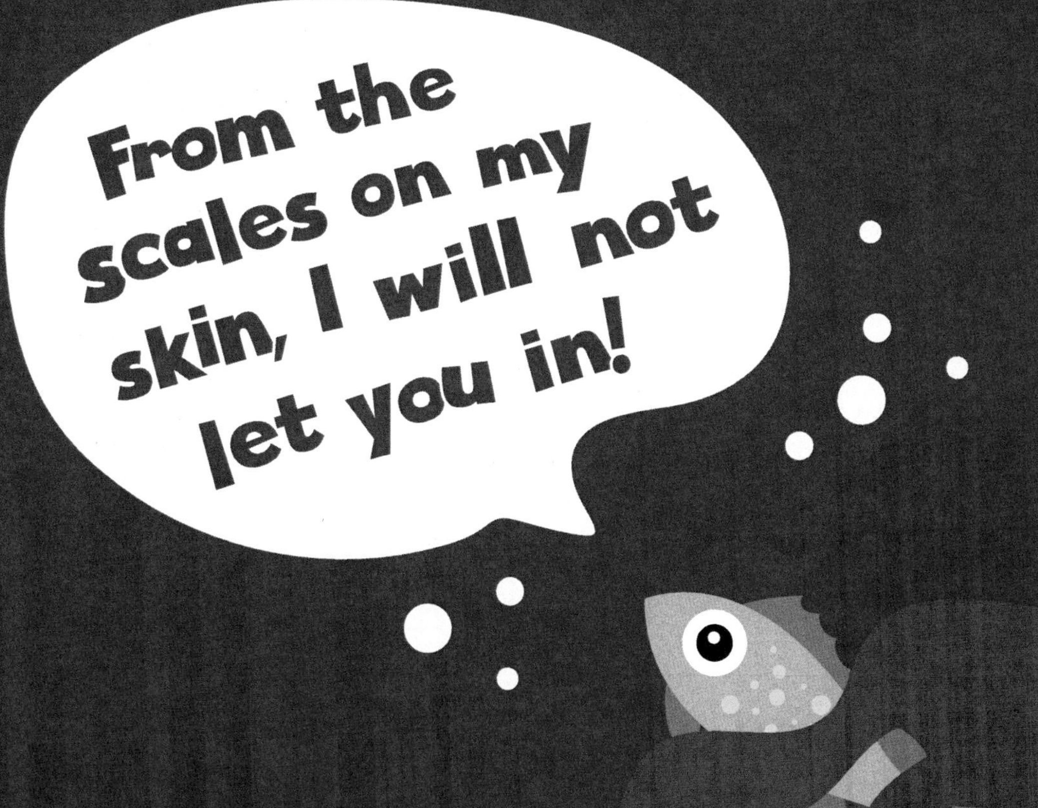

So the **BIG BAD GAR** grumbled...

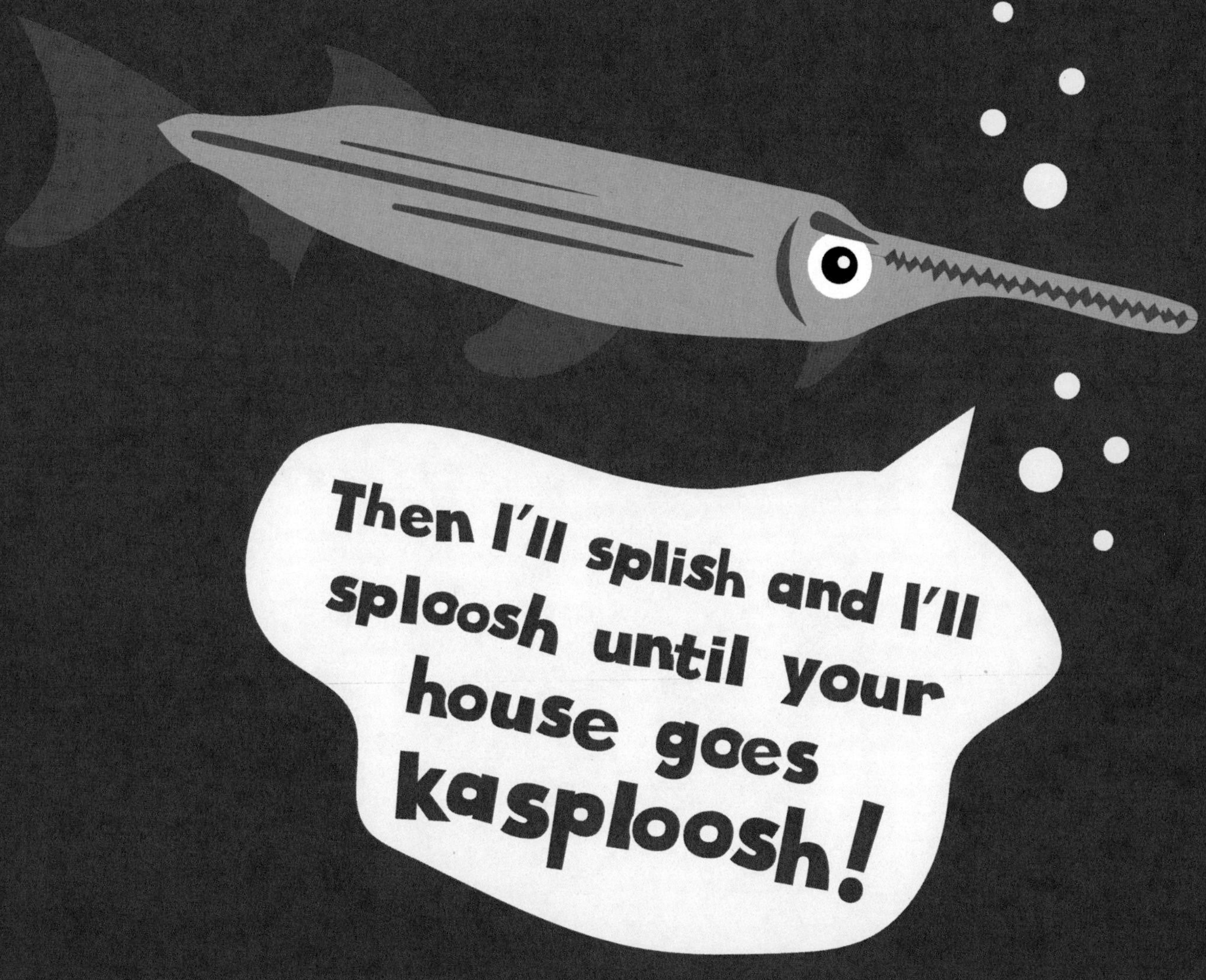

So he splished and he splooshed and the house went kasploosh! And the **BIG BAD GAR** ate little bass number **ONE**.

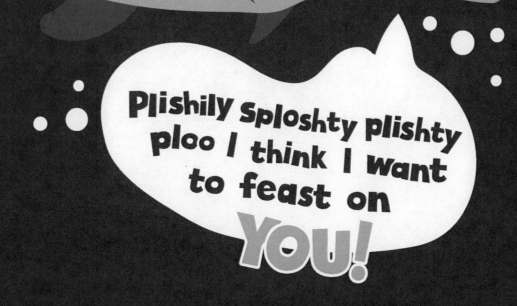

The **BIG BAD GAR** went to bass number **TWO**'s house and growled...

Plishily sploshty plishty ploo I think I want to feast on **YOU!**

Little bass fish number **TWO** answered...

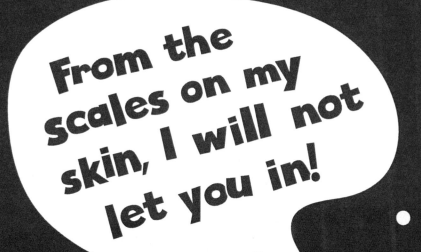

From the scales on my skin, I will not let you in!

So the BIG BAD GAR grumbled...

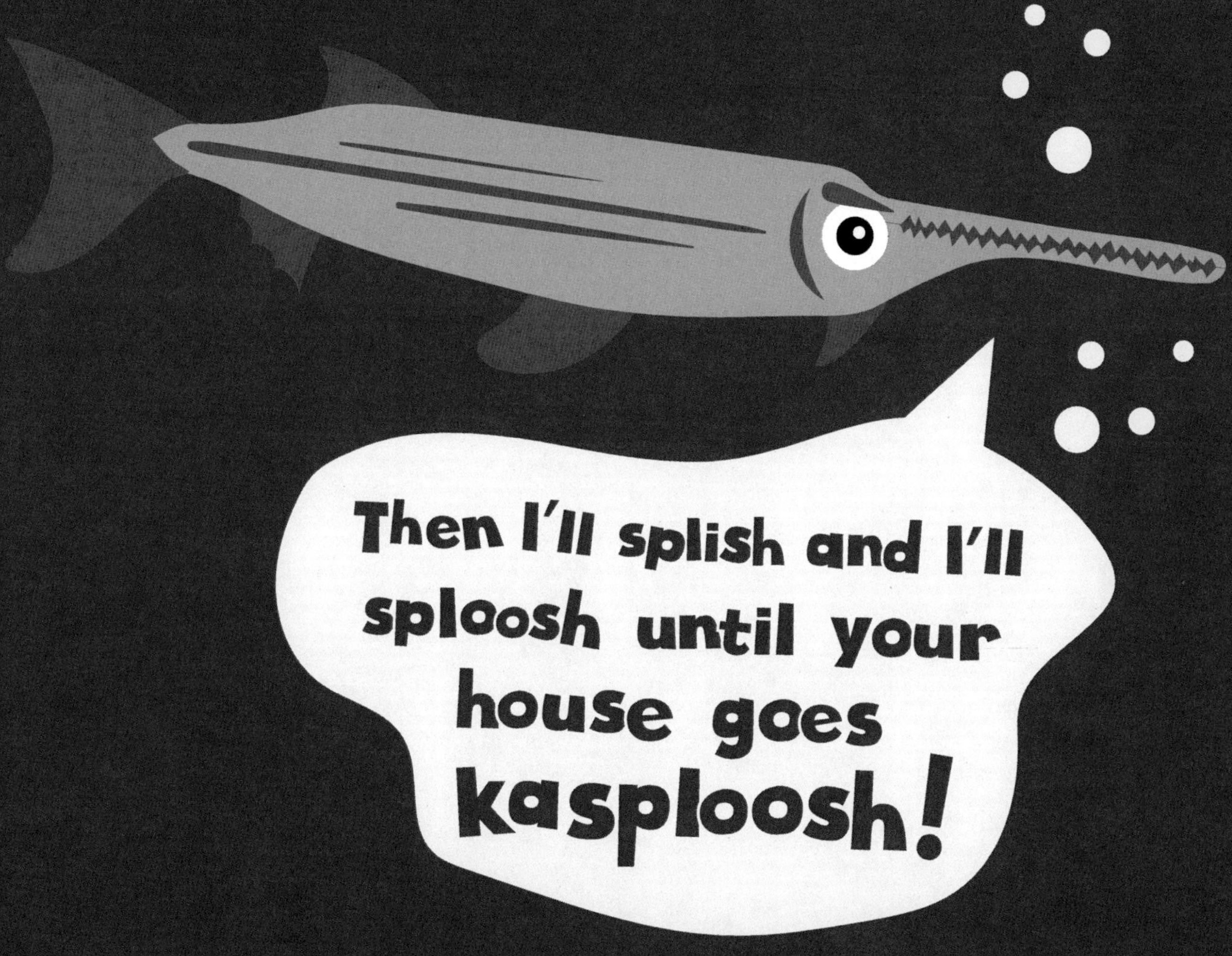

So he splished and he splooshed and the house went kasploosh! And the **BIG BAD GAR** ate little bass number **TWO**.

Then, the **BIG BAD GAR** came to bass number **THREE**'s house and said...

Little bass fish number THREE said...

From the scales on my skin, I will not let you in!

So the **BIG BAD GAR** grumbled...

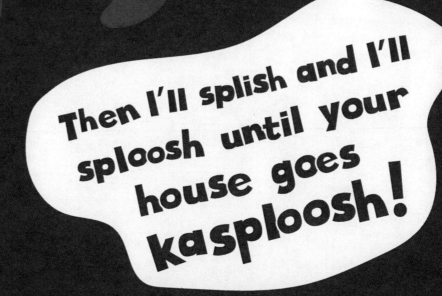

Then I'll splish and I'll sploosh until your house goes **kasploosh!**

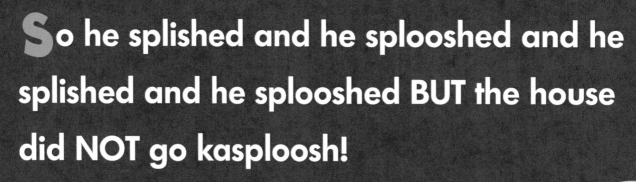

So he splished and he splooshed and he splished and he splooshed BUT the house did NOT go kasploosh!

Little bass number **THREE** came up with a plan. Floating nearby was a fisherman's hook with a tasty worm dangling from it.

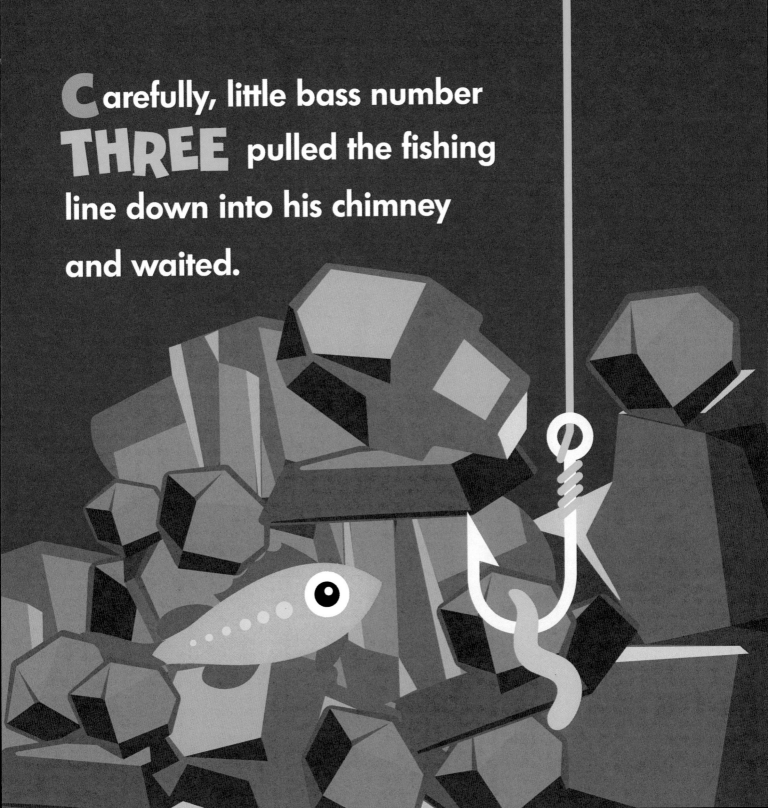

Carefully, little bass number **THREE** pulled the fishing line down into his chimney and waited.

Soon, the **BIG BAD GAR** came back and swam up to the chimney and said...

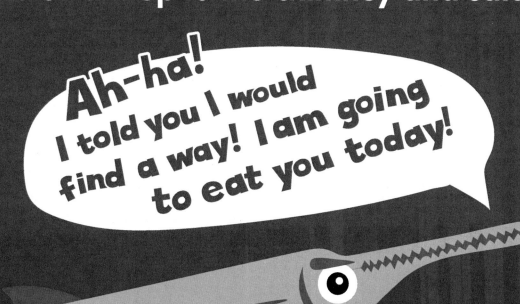

The BIG BAD GAR swam down the chimney and noticed a tasty worm dangling in the water. He was so excited he dove for the worm without noticing the big shiny hook!

Oh boy! Fish tacos tonight!

The **BIG BAD GAR** was hooked! The fisherman felt the tug on his line and quickly reeled him in!

Little bass number **THREE** lived happily ever after in his cozy house of rocks on the bottom of Little Lake Gaston.

THE END

JAMES MILLER

James wrote this story when he was 8 years old. He is now almost 10 and lives with his older brother, Charlie, and his parents in Apex, North Carolina. He loves flag football and math and wants to be a sports analyst when he grows up. James likes collecting football cards and listening to rock and roll.

KRIS TAFT MILLER

James' mom, Kris Taft Miller, is a graphic designer who began her career at Walt Disney Feature Animation. Since 2005, she has had her own graphic design company specializing in everything from logos, websites, books, print projects and more.

ktdesignllc.com • printdesignsbykris.com

Made in the USA
Las Vegas, NV
06 June 2022